For Daniel RR

minedition

North American edition published 2020 by minedition, New York

Michael Neugebauer Publishing Ltd.,
19 West 21st Street, #1201, New York, NY 10010
e-mail: info@minedition.com
This book was printed in May 2020 at Hong Kong Discovery Printing Company Limited.
3/F., Blue Box Factory Building, 25 Hing Wo Street, Tin Wan, Aberdeen, Hong Kong, China
Typesetting in Silentium Pro Roman I
Library of Congress Cataloging-in-Publication Data available upon request.

ISBN 978-1-6626-5006-2
10 9 8 7 6 5 4 3 2 1
First Impression

For more information please visit our website: www.minedition.com

Reynard
THE FOX

Tales from the life of
Reynard the Fox

Retold by RENATE RAECKE
Illustrated by JONAS LAUSTRÖER

minedition

KING NOBLE THE LION
ASSEMBLES HIS SUBJECTS AT WHITSUN

One day – this was at the time when the animals still lived in their own kingdom – Noble the lion, king of all the beasts, called his subjects, as he did every year, to come to a friendly meeting. It was held at Whitsun, the season when nature is beautifully adorned with fresh green birch leaves, and the birds twitter and rejoice from early morning to late at night. For a few days quarrels and fighting, enmity and violence among the animals were forbidden. Peace was to reign among all the creatures of the realm. It was famous as "the king's peace," and for many decades all Noble's subjects had felt safe while that peace lasted. From the smallest mouse to the biggest bear, from the slowest snail to the swiftest hare, all the animals were summoned to the king's court.

King Noble the lion had sent out messengers to every corner of his land with invitations. The annual Whitsun meeting was important to him, because during those days all the animals could tell the king about their anxieties and complaints. And all of them, whether strong or weak, rich or poor, must be able to know that no harm would come to them on their way to the peaceful Whitsun festival. Every animal must be able to ask the king for justice.

Groups of animals had already been arriving at the court for days. The smallest and weakest of them, like hedgehogs, frogs, field mice, and other tiny creatures had set off in good time, so as not to miss the splendid show when the large beasts, the nobility of the animal world, finally made a spectacular entrance at court along a red carpet, with great pomp and ceremony.

Of course the proud and famous creatures of the animal realm, those who were known to everyone, arrived last: Isegrim the wolf, with his wife Lady Greedymind and their children; Bruin the bear with his followers; and Tybalt the cat. They had all staged their late appearance carefully, and enjoyed all the attention. Pardel the panther waved affably to right and left. In his retinue was Lampe the hare, who, to be honest, did not cut a very grand figure. He tried to slink past the spectators in Pardel's shadow.

Grimbert the badger was one of the last to appear. He was not particularly popular, so the applause for him was half-hearted – but when he appeared the animals put their heads together, and there was whispering as rumors went around.

Only one animal was still missing from the royal day of justice: Reynard the fox. He was the worst of all the king's subjects, a liar, deceiver and rogue. He probably guessed that the assembled animals were going to bring charges against him in the royal court of law. And so they did.

ISEGRIM THE WOLF COMPLAINS OF REYNARD THE FOX

When King Noble was seated, with his noble queen enthroned beside him, he gave a sign for the meeting to begin.

Isegrim the wolf was first to come before the king and complain. His complaint, as expected, was of Reynard the fox.

"It would take me a whole week," began Isegrim, with a theatrical gesture, "to tell you everything that Reynard has done to me and my family. He has lied to us and deceived us, beaten us up and robbed us, he has sprayed poisoned water in my children's eyes, leaving them nearly blind, and as for his shameful treatment of my wife Greedymind..."

"Stop, stop! We know that already," said Tybalt the cat. "We all know these stories." Tybalt, who like Bruin the bear had a special place at King Noble's court as one of his closest advisers, could allow himself to interrupt like that.

The animals grew restless, and voices were heard raised here and there. With a lordly gesture, King Noble told them to be silent, because the next petitioner was already coming forward. He too had a complaint to make of that cunning rogue Reynard.

CHANTICLEER THE ROOSTER MOURNS FOR HIS DAUGHTER SCRATCHYCLAW, THE BEST OF ALL EGG-LAYING HENS

Chanticleer the rooster stepped out in the festive meeting-place with a sad flock of followers, attracting the attention of one and all with their miserable crowing and cackling. A stretcher was carried in behind him, and on it lay the hen Scratchyclaw, Chanticleer's daughter, who was famous far and wide as the best of all egg-laying chickens. But she was in a terrible state, poor thing, for her head was missing! Four chickens carried the stretcher, and beside it walked two roosters carrying candles. They were Cockadoodle and Doodledoo, Chanticleer's eldest sons, and they too were known all over the land for their courage and daring.

"It was in spring," Chanticleer the rooster began his tale, "when winter was over and flowers, leaves and green grass were growing and blooming everywhere. Every day of my life, I was glad I had such a large family. My wife had brought up ten sons and twice seven daughters the year before. We were well off; I had nothing to complain of. We lived in safety, well guarded by farm dogs, inside the walls of a monastery, and we wanted for nothing, except perhaps a larger run than the monastery garden where we could scratch about and peck up food.

"But you know what young people are like: they wanted to know what life outside the monastery walls had to offer," Chanticleer went on.

"One day, when we ventured out, Reynard met us, dressed in the robes of a pious monk. He talked about the royal peace that you, wise king, have decreed at Whitsun. And he said that he, Reynard, had changed his way of life and had vowed never to hurt any other animal again. How I wish I had never believed him!"

Chanticleer was fighting back tears. "Reynard set traps for us!" he went on. "When I left the monastery walls with my children, and they were happily and curiously exploring the world beyond our farmyard, Reynard, who was hiding in the bushes, sprang his trap. He barred our way back to the monastery garden, and before the watchdogs could do anything about it he had hunted several of my children to death. Attacking with desperate force, the dogs managed to tear the body of my daughter Scratchyclaw away from him, but she had lost her beautiful head."

Now Chanticleer the rooster turned directly to his king. "I had twenty-four children – now I have only these six left. You see, lord king, how badly Reynard has treated me, you see what trouble I am in. Reynard must be punished for breaking the peace."

King Noble angrily shook his mane. Was Reynard the fox brazen enough to disobey his orders? He could not and would not put up with such a thing.

More and more animals came forward to complain. Pardel the panther, visibly upset, drew Lampe the hare forward.

Pardel the panther and Lampe the hare

"My king," said Pardel the panther, "we all have bad memories of Reynard the fox, each of us has fallen for his nasty tricks several times, but what he was bold enough to do today cannot go unpunished. He broke the peace."

Pardel thrust Lampe the hare forward. "Look at him, lord king," said Pardel the panther. "You see an animal who set out to come here, trusting in your invitation – and what does he look like now?"

What a pitiful sight the hare was! His fur was untidy, and some of it pulled out, he was encrusted with blood from head to foot, there were marks of strangling on his throat, his ears hung down all limp, and there was pure terror in his eyes. Not a word passed his lips.

With difficulty, King Noble suppressed his wrath. "You speak up for Lampe, Pardel, how did this happen?"

"When I was on my way here this morning," Pardel went on, "I heard Reynard's voice in a bush. He was telling Lampe here that he would teach him to sing pious hymns. Hymns? That brought me up short. I stayed where I was and listened.

"'Are you sure you're not planning to do me any harm, Reynard?' I heard Lampe ask cautiously.

"That villain Reynard only laughed. 'Whatever can you be thinking, friend Lampe? You know that our king has decreed peace, so how could anything harm you?'

"'Very well, then,' said Lampe, and he came out of hiding. 'In that case I'd like to learn singing from you.' And he went trustfully towards Reynard."

Pardel the panther found it hard to go on with his story. "Reynard didn't hesitate for a moment. When Lampe was close enough for him to attack, he bit his neck, beat him and shook him – and if I hadn't come leaping out of the bushes to his aid, that would have been the end of Lampe the hare."

Now it was impossible for King Noble to keep his subjects at the assembly calm any longer. They were too angry with Reynard, and they were all demanding justice and drastic punishment for that good-for-nothing fox at the top of their voices.

GRIMBERT THE BADGER DEFENDS REYNARD

"Lord king," Grimbert interrupted, "it has always been the custom at your court for no one to be condemned in his absence. As my honored cousin Reynard has not come here, I would like to speak in his defense, for we all know that there are two sides to every story. If I hear what Isegrim has to say in accusing Reynard, then you must hear me telling you about the nasty trick that Isegrim himself once played on my honored cousin Reynard. A king who claims to do justice must also hear the case for the defense."

King Noble the lion nodded, as a sign that he agreed, and asked the assembly to give the badger a hearing.

THE STORY OF THE FISHMONGER

Grimbert glanced around, to reassure himself that all the animals were looking at him intently, and he gave the queen in particular a winning smile.

"It was in winter weather," he began his plea for the defense, "when all the animals were so hungry that they would have been glad of even a bone gnawed clean, it was then that Isegrim the wolf and my honored cousin Reynard the fox formed an alliance with each other. They agreed to go hunting together," he went on, "to get food for themselves and their families. Everything they caught was to be divided between them honestly and in friendship. Or so at least they agreed.

"One day they saw a fishmonger going to market with his horse and cart. The cart was loaded up with delicious fresh fish, and the scaly skins of the fish glittered in the winter sunlight. Isegrim and Reynard felt their mouths watering – but neither of them had any money to buy his wares from the fishmonger honestly.

"While Isegrim was still lamenting and complaining that his stomach was grumbling, Reynard had already thought up a clever trick. He lay down on the road, right in the fishmonger's way, and played dead.

"The fishmonger, who was suspicious at first, approached the fox with a knife, ready to chase him away at any time, but Reynard played his part perfectly. He lay there, stiff and rigid, and so deceived the fishmonger. 'I have plenty of time,' thought the fishmonger, 'he's dead as a doornail. I can skin him at home and then take his skin to market with me.' So he threw the fox who looked so dead up into his cart, and went on his way to do his other business first.

"While the fishmonger drove on to market, looking ahead of him, Reynard the fox came back to life, and busily threw fish after fish out of the back of the cart and down to his companion Isegrim. Isegrim, who was following the cart at a safe distance, picked them all up just as busily.

"Finally, when the cart was lighter by about half, Reynard felt tired of the work and jumped down, asking Isegrim for his share of the fish.

"'There's your share, and you're welcome to it,' said the wolf, with a cunning grin, pointing to the road behind them – where nothing lay but fishbones gnawed bare. Isegrim had greedily satisfied his hunger without a thought for his friend, although Reynard had thrown down the fish right in front of his nose."

Grimbert paused, seeing that the king and queen were whispering excitedly to each other. He bowed low to the royal pair, and waited in silence for the decision.

King Noble tried to restrain his anger, and talked for a moment to Bruin the bear and Tybalt the cat, his confidential advisers.

Then he announced his verdict. "We will send a messenger to Reynard. He must appear in person to answer the charges against him. Hear me!" said the king, turning to Bruin. "I will entrust that message to you. But beware of his deceiving ways. You have heard yourself what cunning tricks he plays on my subjects."

"Never fear, my king," said Bruin. "I've known about Reynard's sly malice long enough. He won't find it easy to hoodwink me!"

BRUIN THE BEAR IN THE HONEY-TRAP

Bruin set cheerfully off on his way. He felt proud, and at the same time he was sure that he would be able to carry out his task to the satisfaction of the king and the whole assembly.

He walked for three hours or more. The sun was high in the midday sky when he came to the home of Reynard the fox. Over the entrance, it said MALEPARTUS. It was a very grand house, with many branching underground passages, and it showed how prosperous Reynard was.

Bruin knocked on the door – but nothing stirred inside.

"I come in the name of the king!" called Bruin, and he knocked again, hard. "I am to take you to court, Reynard, where you must answer for yourself, because many of the animals have brought charges against you."

Reynard was standing on the other side of the door, and he had heard the knocking perfectly well. He was wondering feverishly how to deal with this situation. He did not in the least want to go to court and listen to the animals' complaints, and he was angry with Bruin the bear for showing off about the importance of his message. Finally, however, he did open the door.

"Noble Bruin, what an honor for me that you have come here in person on the king's behalf!" he said, flattering his guest. "I would have gone to court tomorrow anyway, because I want to give an account of myself there. But I'm sorry to say that I have an upset stomach as a result of over-eating, and I don't feel well today. Stay with me for the night, if you like, and rest after your long journey. Then we can go to court together tomorrow."

Bruin, who was indeed exhausted and hungry after coming such a long way, licked his lips. "May I ask, Reynard, what you've been eating so much of? To be honest, I could do with a bite to eat to give me strength."

"Oh, Bruin, I'm afraid it wasn't the kind of food I can offer a noble-man like you. My wife Ermelin and I had only a couple of miserable fresh honeycombs for our whole family – and it upset our stomachs. I won't be eating honey again in a hurry."

Reynard knew very well that honey was the bear's favorite food.

"Honey?" asked Bruin the bear. "What's so bad about honey? I'd die for honey. If you show me where I can find and enjoy some honey, I'll show my gratitude by standing up for you in front of King Noble."

Reynard pretended to be surprised. "You really like that sticky stuff? Well, if that's so, then I can show you where to get more than enough of it. Lantfert the carpenter lives half a mile from here, and he has as much honey on his farm as anyone could want."

Reynard ran on ahead and Bruin followed him. "Bruin won't forget this honey banquet for a long time," thought Reynard spitefully.

They waited until evening came. The trunk of an oak tree was lying in the carpenter's yard, because he meant to make it into furniture. It was already split in half lengthwise, and Lantfert had driven two wedges into the split to right and left to keep it open.

"There's more honey than you could eat in this split tree trunk," Reynard told Bruin. "If you feel far enough inside, you'll find it. But go carefully, and don't eat too much. Think of our journey back to court tomorrow."

Bruin the bear, in his greed, wasn't even listening any more as he dug his forepaws deep into the split trunk. Reynard used that moment to strike the wedges out of the trunk with a mighty blow. The split in the trunk closed – and Bruin was caught. He began raging and roaring, he cursed Reynard and he cursed his own stupidity. He tried with all his might to pull his paws out of the split trunk, but in vain.

Lantfert, woken by all the noise, came out into the yard. When he saw the bear in the trap, he ran to the village inn for reinforcements. Sticks and clubs, muck forks and rakes, even a rolling pin came down on poor Bruin's back, making him writhe in pain. In his time of need, fear gave him fresh strength; he managed to free his paws, but some of his coat stayed stuck in the tree. He ran from the furious crowd into the dark.

Reynard, who had watched all this from a distance, set off happily for home. Once again he had found a way of teaching an opponent a lesson by means of a cunning trick.

GREEDYMIND COMPLAINS OF REYNARD

While all at court were waiting for Bruin's return, Isegrim's wife Lady Greedymind had made her way before the king.

"Oh noble, high and wise king," she said, "I know it is not the custom here for women to speak in their own cause." She cast a pleading glance at the queen. "But as your adviser Tybalt cut my husband short so roughly at the beginning of this assembly, I beg your permission to tell you myself what Reynard did to me."

King Noble felt his wife's paw gently pressing his arm – and he nodded to Greedymind. "Go on, then, tell your tale!"

REYNARD TEACHES GREEDYMIND TO FISH

"One day," began Greedymind, "in a bitterly cold, frosty winter, I met Reynard on the banks of a frozen lake. We were both feeling cross and discontented, for we hadn't found anything much to eat for days – and everyone knows that hunger makes you bad-tempered.

"Reynard, however, was acting as if he had just eaten a lavish, delicious meal. He patted his belly with a growl of pleasure. 'What pity you didn't turn up earlier, Lady Greedymind,' said the rogue, hypocritically. 'I'd have been happy to share my fish dish with you – there was too much for me on my own anyway.'"

Now Greedymind wrung her paws and could hardly restrain her tears. "It was a terrible moment; I was trembling with hunger and cold. 'Where did you get the fish?' I was quick to ask. 'I haven't found anything for me and the children to eat for days.'

"Now Reynard acted the part of a generous friend – and if I hadn't been so desperately anxious about my children, I'd probably have seen through his trick much sooner. 'Come out on the ice with me,' he said. 'It's perfectly simple to catch fish; the lake is full of them.'

"When Reynard had scratched a hole in the ice, he told me, 'Sit down here, hang your tail in the water, and you'll soon see that you have more fish on your line than you and your children can eat.'

"My need made me credulous, and I failed to see Reynard's crafty expression, although I had learnt so often that he was a sly deceiver.

"I did as he said because I was so hungry. Reynard also advised me to be patient, and not to take my tail out of the water too soon. 'Good things take time,' he said.

"I noticed only too late that Reynard had been fooling me. I felt my tail getting heavier and heavier, but when I tried to stretch my stiff limbs and lift my catch out of the water, the hole in the ice was frozen over.

"Reynard had just been waiting for this moment, and once again he acted out of spite: as he ran swiftly away he made such a loud noise that the villagers noticed and came out on the ice with clubs and poles to kill me. I fought desperately, and in the end I lost a good part of my tail as I freed myself from the ice with a painful jerk. If my faithful Isegrim hadn't come to my aid, I'd have been in mortal fear for my life."

Greedymind fell silent, and with a bashful expression showed the ragged end of her once beautiful tail.

The queen was obviously moved, and the king promised the she-wolf that this nasty trick of Reynard's should not go unavenged either.

BRUIN'S RETURN

Meanwhile, Bruin was on his laborious way back. All his limbs hurt, and some of his wounds were bleeding. Exhausted and maltreated as he was, it took him many more hours to come before the king again than he had needed to reach Reynard's earth. He was a picture of misery.

The king was beside himself with rage to see him. "Has Reynard treated my finest nobleman, my closest adviser so shamefully? On my honor and my crown, he will pay for it." Another council of state was held in a hurry. The law said that an accused criminal must be summoned to a court of law a second and a third time before a verdict could be passed on him. It was decided to send Tybalt the cat to Reynard this time.

"My gracious king," begged Tybalt, "if Bruin, who is so big and strong, could do nothing, how can I hope to bring Reynard here?"

"You may be small but you have a clever head," said the king, "and you know all about wily cunning. I am sure you'll succeed. Use your wits!"

Tybalt the cat won't leave the mice alone, and regrets it bitterly

When Tybalt came to Malepartus, the fox's earth, Reynard was sitting outside the door basking in the afternoon sun. The cat gave him a civil greeting and said at once, as he had been instructed, "Listen to me, Reynard! The king sends me to tell you that you are to return to court with me immediately. If you refuse, it will be the worse for you and your whole family."

Reynard smiled a honey-sweet smile. "Welcome, Tybalt! Rest first; you have come a long way, and evening is falling. Why not stay the night, and we can set off first thing tomorrow morning?"

The fox was trying to gain time, for he had no intention of going back to court with Tybalt.

Tybalt tried to stand his ground. "No, there's no reason to wait. There will be a clear sky tonight with the light of the moon and stars. We can set out at once."

"Why run risks?" replied Reynard. "There are many shady characters on the move after dark, and you never know who can be trusted." And who knew that better than Reynard himself?

Tybalt weakened. "But what will we eat tonight if we stay here?"

Reynard had just been waiting for that question. "Well, you'll have to be content with our own simple supper. Today we're having delicious fresh honeycombs."

"Ugh, no thank you! Now a nice fat mouse would be a different matter."

Reynard pretended to be surprised. "Are you serious? If that's all, there's a barn where the mice dance at night, next to the pastor's house beside the duckpond that you passed on your way. We have a real plague of mice here!"

That rascal Reynard had broken a hole in the barn wall days ago, and he had been through it several times to steal chickens. He knew that now the pastor had set a trap in the form of a noose just inside the hole to catch the chicken thief.

"Off you go, then," he told Tybalt. "The barn is over there. Wait a moment; don't you hear the mice squealing, and the rustling sound as they run about? Go in, and I'll stay on watch outside. Then in the morning, when you've eaten your fill, we'll set out."

Tybalt didn't hesitate for long before he disappeared through the hole, and ran right into the trap. Soon after that, he could be heard mewing pitifully and calling for help. As for Reynard, who had known just what would happen in advance, he made fun of him outside the barn, wished him a good appetite, and danced cheerfully away.

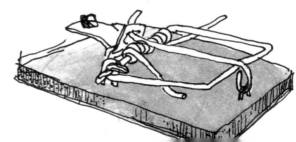

But the pastor had heard the noise. Suspecting that he had caught the chicken thief, he woke his family and the servants, armed them all with cudgels, broomsticks, cooking spoons and shovels, and led them into the barn.

Tybalt, who had felt the nose tightening more firmly round his neck with every movement that he made, screamed in sheer terror – but the blows rained down on him. In panic, he leaped at the pastor's face and dug all his claws in to defend himself. With a howl, the pastor stopped and then fell to the floor as if paralyzed. Tybalt used that moment of general confusion to bite through the noose, and he fled through the hole in the barn wall, groaning, and out into the night.

TYBALT'S RETURN

They were waiting impatiently at court for Tybalt's return. When he stood before them, with his fur all tousled, one ear missing, a swollen eye, and the remains of the noose still round his neck, a horrified silence reigned.

King Noble's anger was terrible. Two of his best followers had been tricked and humiliated by Reynard. He must be condemned, so much was clear, but how could he be brought here? Who would risk his life to be a messenger this time?

GRIMBERT OFFERS TO BRING REYNARD TO COURT

Grimbert the badger, who had already promised to defend the fox, rose. "My king, many have gathered here to lay their complaints against Reynard. I can't deny that he has a bad reputation. However, the principle still holds good that if the king listens to the case for the prosecution, then Reynard the fox must also be allowed to defend himself. He has been at liberty until now, and has advised you at court many times, like his father before him. Your laws do not allow us to condemn anyone who has no chance of justifying his actions here. If you like, my king, I myself will bring Reynard to court. As you know, we are related, and he will listen to me."

King Noble was visibly relieved to hear Grimbert offering to go of his own free will. "Your proposal is a good one, Grimbert; I trust your wisdom and foresight. But there will be no more excuses! He must answer for himself here, and if he will not come willingly then we must bring him by force."

Grimbert bowed, thanked the king for his trust in him, and gave the queen another winning smile. He knew how fond she was of Reynard, in spite of all the complaints against him.

GRIMBERT BRINGS REYNARD TO COURT

So Grimbert set off to where Reynard lived. When he came to the fox's earth, Reynard and his wife Ermelin were both sitting outside the door, watching two fox cubs playing in the evening sunlight.

"Grimbert, my friend," said Reynard, "welcome to Malepartus! You know my wife Ermelin – and those are my two promising sons Rossel and Reinhart who, I hope, will do honor to their father's name some day. Be our guest this evening!"

Grimbert did not waste time on polite excuses. "Friend Reynard, much as I would like to stay with you we have no time. The king has sent for you twice already – why must you always go too far? I can't defend you at court any longer if you won't appear in person. You have supported the king many times, with words and deeds, and he has listened to your advice in difficult situations. Why do you defy him now when there's no need for it, and you know that things may end badly for you? You must come back with me at once, or there'll be no more I can do for you and your family. If you don't follow me now, the king will send his soldiers…"

Reynard didn't hesitate for long. "I'll take your advice. I know I can trust you." Then he embraced his wife, gave her the key to the gate, and begged her fervently to take good care of Rossel and Reinhart.

"You know," he said, "that they mean everything to me, they are my pride and joy!" Ermelin nodded. Did she really have to remind him that they were her sons too?

Reynard wouldn't have heard what she said in any case, for he was already on the road with Grimbert. He seemed to be in good humor and certain of victory, and he chatted as if they were going to a convivial party. "We'll do as you advised me, Grimbert, that will be best. After all, I have nothing to fear – I have often been a good adviser to the king."

"The king and the people want to see you hanged. I hope you can still save your neck from the noose," said Grimbert. "You have broken the king's peace many times, you have mistreated Lampe, Bruin and Tybalt. And Isegrim will present the case for the prosecution – it won't be easy for you."

"Just leave it to me." Reynard did not seem downcast. "The king has often listened to my good advice. If I can just have a few words with him and the queen, I am sure to think of something."

At court, they were already saying that the fox was on his way with Grimbert, and the number of angry people laying charges against him grew by the hour. Large and small alike, they ran to the meeting place to see Reynard the fox face his royal judge at long last.

Reynard, accompanied by Grimbert, looked cheerful, greeted acquaintances right and left with a joke, shook the hands that were offered here and there, and ignored the many fists being shaken at him. His adversaries did not all seem to feel the same.

So he stepped forward, bowing to the royal couple, and acting now modestly, now boastfully.

"Lord king, noble queen, here I am. A little late, to be sure, but important family reasons kept me away. I understand that I am to be put on trial here today. Well, I know you are a just king, Noble, and so I will give a full account of myself."

King Noble, who had already seen the show that Reynard put on for the crowd with suppressed anger, rose and roared, "Silence – see how you have treated my faithful Bruin and Tybalt, and hear Isegrim's complaints!"

"Well, all I can say about your envoys Bruin and Tybalt is this: their own greed deafened them to my good advice. Instead of showing moderation, as I had recommended Bruin to do in view of the journey back that was before us, he couldn't stuff his throat full enough, and he fell on those honeycombs without restraint. I couldn't guess that he would take so little care, and wouldn't be strong enough to resist temptation.

"As for Tybalt, I invited him to share a simple supper with me and my family. Instead, he insisted on going off to hunt mice. How could I know that he, a cat, would go about it so stupidly that he would wake even the pastor, who usually sleeps the sleep of the just?"

Reynard cleared his throat, passed his paw over his muzzle, and scratched behind his ear. He knew how effective pauses can be.

"And then there's Isegrim," he went on, "who, as I hear from Grimbert, is talking grandly here at court. You know, my king, that there was once friendship between Isegrim and me. And I know from Grimbert that he told the story of the fishmonger here at court.

Tell me, wouldn't I have just as good a right to be considered the injured party in this case? I had the brilliant idea! I threw the fish down at his paws – and in the end I never had a look-in, because Isegrim didn't hold to our agreement. He ate our loot all by himself!"

Reynard looked challengingly into the wolf's face – and was pleased to see that Isegrim didn't meet his gaze.

"My king, noble queen!" Reynard went on. "Allow me to tell you another story in defense of myself. After all, this is a matter of life or death for me!"

The queen nodded even before the king could say anything. So Noble, with a brief gesture of his paw, signed to Reynard to go on.

THE TALE OF THE PRICE OF A FOAL

"One day, in cold, dry spring weather after a long frosty period, Isegrim and I were out together again, hunting for food to nourish our families." Reynard seemed to shiver at the thought of that time. "We'd been searching for prey for a long time, wandering far and wide through this land. I was still walking briskly enough, but Isegrim was limping across country as best he could. And there was no prospect of a nice juicy bit of meat anywhere in sight.

"Unexpectedly – we could hardly believe our eyes – a mare with her foal crossed our path. 'They're heaven-sent,' I murmured. The mare wasn't in her prime any more, but the foal was a charming, not to say an appetizing sight. Isegrim felt too weak to fight, but his mouth was watering.

"'Go to the mare and ask her if she will sell us the young foal, and what its price would be,' begged Isegrim. 'I'm dying of starvation.' He knew my skill in driving a bargain.

"So I went up to the mare and politely asked the price of her foal. The mare raised her newly shod back hoof slightly. 'You want to know the price? Look under my hoof, it's written there.'

"Well, I wouldn't be Reynard the fox if I hadn't seen through the mare's ruse. But how could I warn my partner Isegrim without spoiling his chance of doing a good deal? 'I'm not the one asking the question,' I told the mare. 'It's my friend Isegrim who wants to know the price.'

"'The wolf, is it?' asked the mare. 'Well, so much the better. Tell him to come over here and read the price!'

"I went back to Isegrim and urged him to abandon his idea of driving a bargain. 'The price could be far too high, and for all I know you won't even be able to read it,' I warned him.

"Now as you know, my king, Isegrim thinks highly of his good education, which is much better than mine.

"'Why wouldn't I be able to read the price?' he snapped. 'I'm not letting this deal escape me, you fool!' There was no stopping Isegrim now. He dragged himself over to the mare, discussed the purchase of the foal with her again, and then bent low over her raised hoof.

"What was bound to happen did happen. With a well-aimed kick in the face, the mare knocked Isegrim to the ground. He lay unconscious at my feet for an hour – and by then the mare and her foal were over the hills and far away.

"I had been wasting my breath when I warned him, something that happens with so much of my good advice. I suppose I'm the fool really, but I am not standing here to accuse anyone, although I too have suffered harm."

Reynard paused again, and looked expectantly at the king. Here and there some of the animals clapped, and a few words of approval rang out over the meeting place.

The queen bent over to Noble. "Of course the decision is yours alone, my dear. But I like what Reynard says. Everything suggests that he has a clever mind. Can you really afford to do without his sharp wits here at court? Perhaps he may yet be useful to you now and then."

King Noble had not expected the fox to speak with such courteous modesty. Against his will, he was impressed, and he sensed that the voices raised in the assembly to accuse the fox were not so loud now.

"Reynard," said the king, "you have spoken boldly and frankly before this assembly. I cannot clear you of all blame, but I see that you have appeared here at court honestly and with your head held high. As king, I need clever minds around me. We will drop the charges against you, and from now on you shall be one of my closest advisers – on one condition: the king's peace must be observed!"

Reynard took care to show none of the triumph that he felt. He bowed to King Noble and knelt before the queen. "Thank you," he said simply, and he turned to go, without even condescending to glance at Isegrim, Bruin and Tybalt.

Reynard on his way home

Before he left the meeting place, the fox shook paws with Grimbert again. "Thank you for your support, my friend," he said. "I won't forget it! Come and see us again some day soon. You know that you are always welcome."

And now Reynard was suddenly in a hurry to get home. "This calls for celebration," he thought, as he trotted happily through the undergrowth. "My family really deserves a lavish meal in honor of this day. A good, well fattened goose would be delicious, but my prospects of finding one at this time of year are poor. So why not stroll home by way of the pastor's duck pond and take a few of the tender young ducks home with me? Ermelin will be glad of them, not to mention Rossel and Reinhart."

No sooner said than done. And so there was pure joy in Malepartus that evening, as the fox's family celebrated Reynard's new rank at court with a dinner of tender duck breasts.

AFTERWORD

The cunning fox made his first appearance in literature in the age of classical antiquity, in Aesop's Fables (c. 550 BC), which are still known to us.

In these short fables, the fox was only one of many animals intended to amuse listeners or readers. The wolf also played a part in the stories (as the fox's antagonist), as well as the dog and the raven, the mouse and the lion, the ant and the grasshopper, to name only a few. Human qualities (for instance vanity, laziness, stupidity, etc.) were illustrated by the behavior of animal characters, narrated in short episodes that always ended with a moral lesson.

It was not until the Middle Ages (c. AD 1150) that a Flemish poet, Magister Nivardus, turned the separate fables into a coherent animal epic, with the wolf as the central character and the fox as his antagonist. The poet gave the animals human characters and individual names, many of which have been retained to this day with slight modifications.

Several versions influenced by the Flemish text appeared in France in the following decades, although they placed the fox at the centre of the story, and celebrated his amusing victories over his enemies' stupidity. The French Roman de Renart (c. 1200) was the beginning of Reynard's fame. It was so successful that the name of the fox, Renart, entirely replaced the old word for a fox, "goupil," in the French language. From now on the French for a fox was, and still is, "un renard."

From that point we can trace the fox's literary travels all over Europe. His cunning intrigues became popular in translations and new versions, for instance in England, Alsace and Flanders. The authors, not all of whom are known to us by name, sometimes placed the emphasis on the fox's amusing tricks, sometimes on satirical descriptions of the church and the clergy, courtly life and worldly power.

In 1498 Reynke de vos, written in Low German, appeared in north Germany. In his text, the anonymous author presented a social system in which the clever fox, despite his misdeeds, wins the highest honors at court. For all his deceitful ways, the eponymous hero Reynke never loses the reader's sympathy. We suffer with his victims, but we smile at the quick wits that enable him to make his escape from apparently hopeless situations. He is a ne'er-do-well whom we despise, and yet at the same time a rascal who is bound to win our admiration. In this, he is in fact very like his literary contemporary, Till Eulenspiegel.

Many new editions of a later High German version were sold at the book fairs of the times, and there were also translations into Danish, Swedish and Latin. A successful book, or what today we would call a best-seller!

Finally, the material also fascinated the most famous of all German poets, Johann Wolfgang von Goethe, who in 1793/1794 wrote a verse epic, Reineke Fuchs, that is part of the classical canon of literature.

This edition presents several well-known stories about Reynard the fox, a heute "hero" of European literature, retold and newly illustrated.

During my childhood and schooldays Reynard was still one of those literary figures whom we all knew. Since then his literary journeys have fallen in number; he has practically disappeared from school textbooks and anthologies, at least in his popular character of a lovable rogue.

For this retelling in 2012, I have made use freely of the various versions of the stories of the fox available to me, exchanging some of the roles, laying more emphasis on some of the voices. And I have not let Reynard perish on the gallows, but allowed him an impudent celebration with his family of his rise in the world. He has been escaping the noose for centuries – I have let him survive in my own version.

Fools and rogues are threatened with extinction – so we ought to remember one of the greatest of their kind.

Renate Raecke